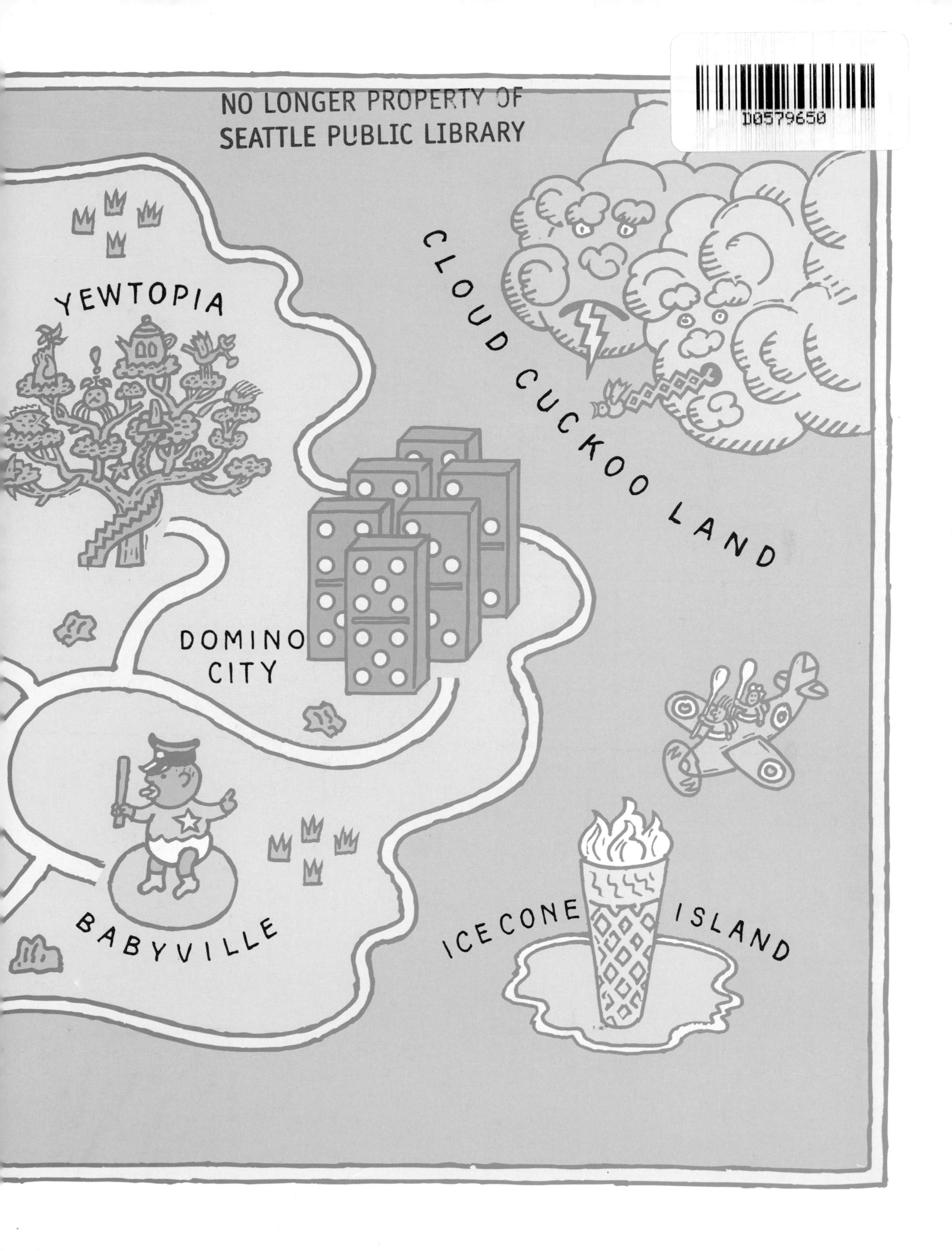

CLOUD CUCKOO LAND
YEWTOPIA
DOMINO
CITY
BABYVILLE
ICECONE ISLAND

Cloud Cuckoo Land

For Louis

Walter Lorraine Books

First Houghton Mifflin edition 1999
Originally published in Great Britain in 1999
Published by arrangement with Egmont Children's Books
239 Kensington High Street, London W8 6SA

Library of Congress Cataloging-in-Publication Data

Lodge, Bernard

Cloud Cuckoo Land/ by Bernard Lodge
p. cm.
Summary: The reader takes a rhyming trip to places not on many maps including Hairland, The Hanging Hills, Ice Cone Island, and Yewtopia.
ISBN: 0-395-96318-4
[1. Voyages and travel — Fiction. 2. Humorous stories. 3. Stories in rhyme.] I. Title.
PZ8.3.L824c1 1999 99-18698
[E] — dc21 CIP

Printed in UAE by Oriental Press Limited

NO LONGER PROPERTY OF
SEATTLE PUBLIC LIBRARY

(And Other Odd Spots)

BERNARD LODGE

HOUGHTON MIFFLIN COMPANY BOSTON 1999

Walter Lorraine Books

Cloud Cuckoo Land

If only I could understand
The place they call Cloud Cuckoo Land.
How do they manage to create
The mountains that are featherweight?
Why are some clouds mean and rotten,
Others pink, like candy cotton?

Tell me why there's so much rain,
And why the angels don't complain.
No! Cuckoo Land is not for me,
Because the greatest mystery,
Is why cloud cuckoos are so rare.
I never saw one anywhere!

Ice Cone Island

Fly to Ice Cone Island
And your tongue will loop the loop,
As you savour every flavour
And explore each double scoop.

Volcanoes splutter chocolate chips,
So don't forget your spoon.
But catch an early plane because
The island melts at noon.

Planet Zero

Whoever goes to Planet Zero,
Has to be a nut or hero:
Lousy weather, lousy food,
It put me in a lousy mood.
And then this alien shook its head,
It gave a bug-eyed look and said,
"Yuck, yuck! I wonder who gave birth
To this weird thing from Planet Earth?

Maybe they are hatched from eggs?
It could explain the two short legs.
And is that tiny mouth for real?
However does it eat a meal?"
"Shove off!" I said, "That's quite enough!"
(I may be tiny but I'm tough.)
"You bugs may think you own the place,
But please don't bug the human race!"

The Sea of Socks

Beware! Beware! The Sea of Socks!
Avoid each woolly wave.
Whoever sails The Sea of Socks
Must be extremely brave.
Like Captain Billy Barnacle,
The bravest man I knew,
Who somehow crossed the darned old socks
Alone, in an open shoe.

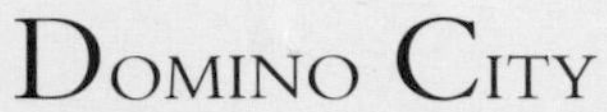

Domino City

Domino City is not very pretty,
For most of it's covered in spots.
And the poor who have blanks get no help from the banks,
While the spottier rich can get lots.

Though some may have many, and some hardly any,
The number of spots doesn't matter.
If the dominoes fall,
Then look out - one and all!
As the city comes down with a clatter.

Hairland

Have you ever been across the sea to Hairland?
Have you ever watched the bushy bristles grow?

Then you must have seen the Wee Folk from Killarney,
As they gently push their mowers to and fro.

The Junkle

The Junkle is a creepy place,
Where creepers never grow.
I used to take my junk in there,
So that is how I know.

And every time I stepped inside,
I took a special map,
To guide me through the undergrowth
Of tangled, rusty scrap.

But now my map is useless,
As the Junkle spreads each day,
And someone somewhere in the world
Finds more to throw away.

Babyville

Babyville is hard to find.
It isn't very large.
That crazy place where a mighty race
Of babies is in charge.
There are baby teachers, baby cops.
The babies run the banks and shops.

And everything from mending shoes,
To covering the TV news.
A baby judge will jail you
If you do not drive with care.
And don't complain to City Hall,
They have a baby mayor!

Cave of Yawn

Roll up and see the Cave of Yawn,
The yawn that lasts from dusk to dawn.
From east to west, and north to south,
You cannot find a bigger mouth.
At 9pm it opens wide,
So make a line to go inside.

You're free to photograph the view,
As tourists always like to do.
But please be quiet, please behave.
Don't throw down litter in the cave.
For if you do, the teeth will SNAP
And catch you in the tourist trap.

The Upside Downs

They're often called The Hanging Hills
Or else The Upside Downs.
And if you think the hills are daft,
You ought to see the towns.

I heard the place was very odd
But then I saw one day,
The sunset setting upwards
And I had to get away.

Yewtopia

Long live Yewtopia
The land of the free!
Although we know it's not on land,
But stuck up in a tree.

A mighty yew tree stretching wide,
And in those leafy heights,
A lemon sole sings soulfully
For seven days and nights.

Come see the busy spider-clock,
Who's always running fast,
It races only with itself,
But always comes in last.

And listen to the trumpet bird,
Who plays the bossa nova.
He plays it to a porcupine
Who sneezes when it's over.

But if the treetop mania
Is more than you can take.
Remember - those who fall asleep,
Can also fall awake.

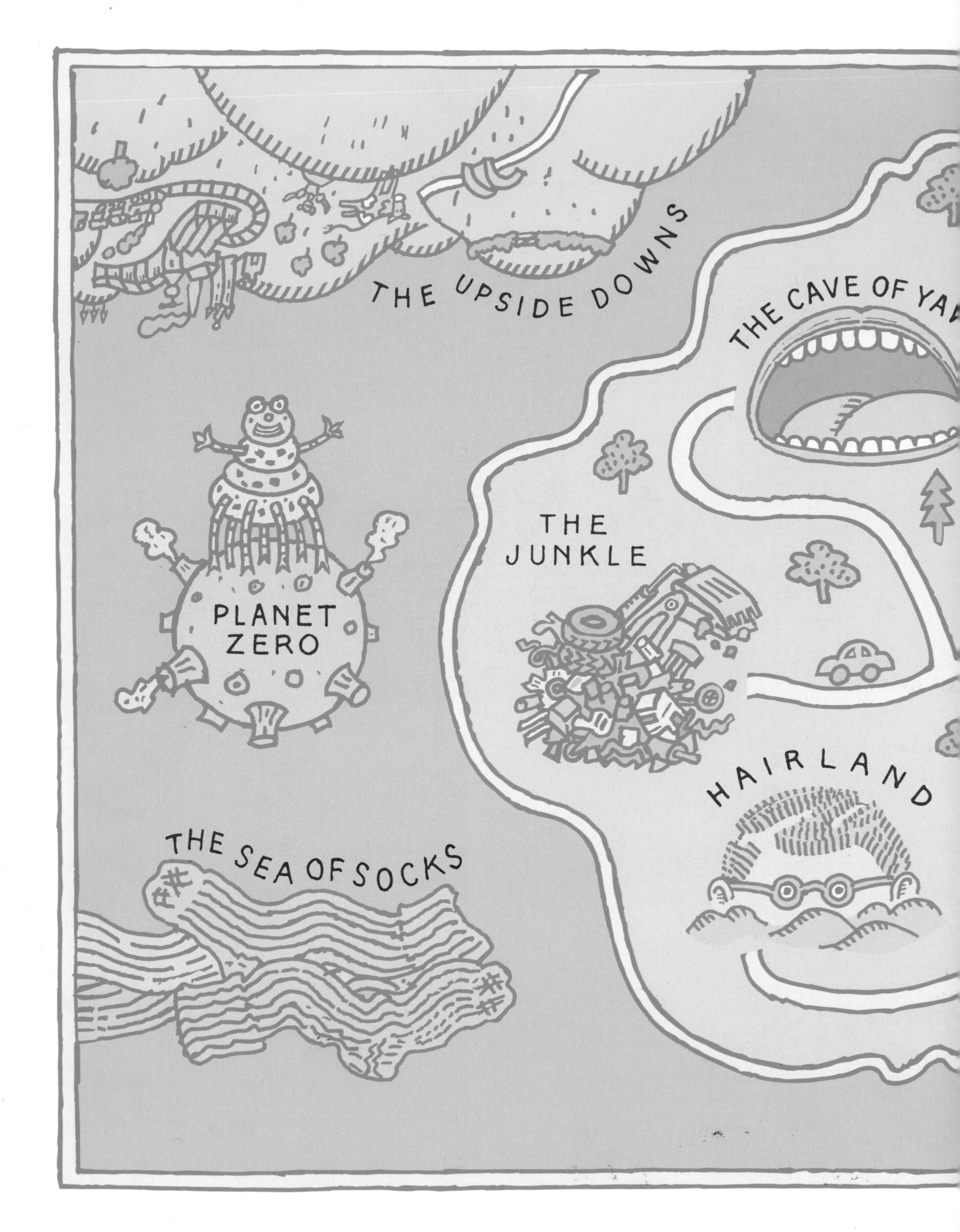
THE UPSIDE DOWNS
THE CAVE OF YA
PLANET ZERO
THE JUNKLE
HAIRLAND
THE SEA OF SOCKS